Y0-CBV-773

The Secret to Teddy's Happiness

David Conway

illustrated by

Dubravka Kolanovic

SANDY CREEK

For Ellie
D.C.

To Marko
D.K.

First published in 2008 in Great Britain by
Gullane Children's Books

Text © David Conway 2008
Illustrations © Dubravka Kolanovic 2008

This 2008 edition published by Sandy Creek
by arrangement with Gullane Children's Books

All rights reserved. No part of this publication may be reproduced, stored
in a retrieval system, or transmitted in any form or by any means, electronic, mechanical,
photocopying, recording or otherwise, without prior permission.

Sandy Creek
122 Fifth Avenue
New York, NY 10011

ISBN-13: 978-1-4351-0920-9

1   3   5   7   9   10   8   6   4   2

Printed and bound in Indonesia

One night, while all the house was sleeping, the toys in the
playroom discovered an old abandoned bear that the children had found.
His fur was matted and his ears were worn. He looked like the most
bedraggled and unhappy teddy bear that ever was.

The toys cleaned him up and found the bear some clothes.
They made a small bed out of whatever they could
find, and set it by the toy box in the playroom.

But despite all their efforts there was a problem. The shabby old bear seemed just as sad as when they had found him. "It's his heart," said the giraffe, "it's broken. That bear needs more than clothes and a comfortable bed to sleep in. He needs to feel happy again."

So that night as moonlight filled the whole room,
the toys embarked on a quest, to go and find the secret,
the secret to Teddy's happiness.

They caught a train,

and then a plane . . .

. . . and sailed on a carpet sea.

They searched the playroom and rummaged around.
But they could not find the secret. No secret could be found.

Then the friends encountered a rabbit who knew everything there was to know, from the height of the tallest building, to where the snow goes when it's not winter.

But the little velvet rabbit had longed for
one thing since the day it was fashioned and sewn.
"I will tell you the secret," said the kind little rabbit,
"if you bring me a star of my own."

So the adventurous toys went in
search of a star in a rickety old toy car.

They found some hanging in the baby's room,
attached by strings to a luminous moon.
"I will give you a star," whispered the moon, "but then,
you must shine a light upon me so I can glimmer again."

So the brave little toys went in search of a light
as all the clocks in the house struck midnight . . .

They found one on an island by a shabby
old lion, but the lion wanted something in return.

"It is cold on this island," said the sleepy old lion, in a
slow and slumberous yawn. "But I will give you this light
if you bring me a scarf that will keep me nice and warm."

So the monkey, the robot,
the raccoon and the giraffe
set off in the moonlight
to search for a scarf . . .

. . . along the dark
murky hallway . . .

. . . down a mountain steep . . .

. . . where they found one piled up
with some coats in a heap.

Then the party of friends returned to the island
and wrapped the scarf around the lion's mane . . .

. . . they shone the light upon the luminous
moon to make it glow and glimmer again.

They flew to the bookshelf on a rocket ship
where the little velvet rabbit lived all alone . . .

. . . and presented it with a tiny star,
one it could call its own.

Then the rabbit revealed the secret
and with an air of cheerfulness,
uttered three tiny words into
the shadowy gloom –
the secret to Teddy's happiness.

So they caught a train . . .

. . . then a plane . . .

. . . and sailed the whole night through,
with three tiny words for a sad old bear,
three magical words . . .

...we love you.